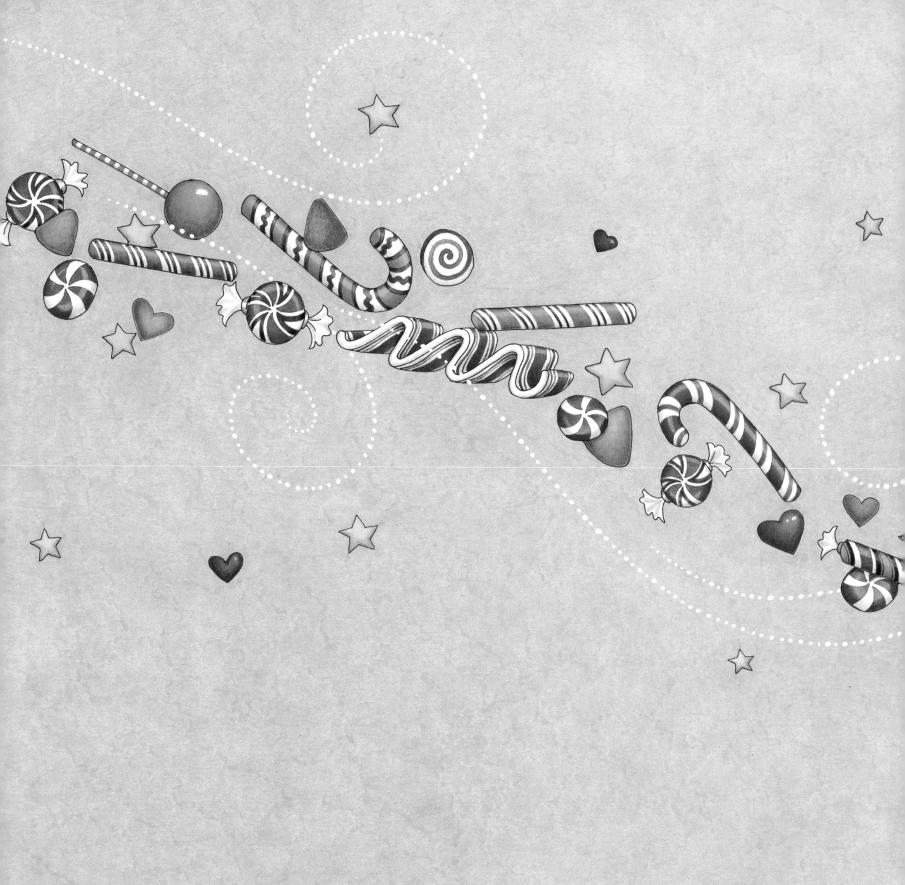

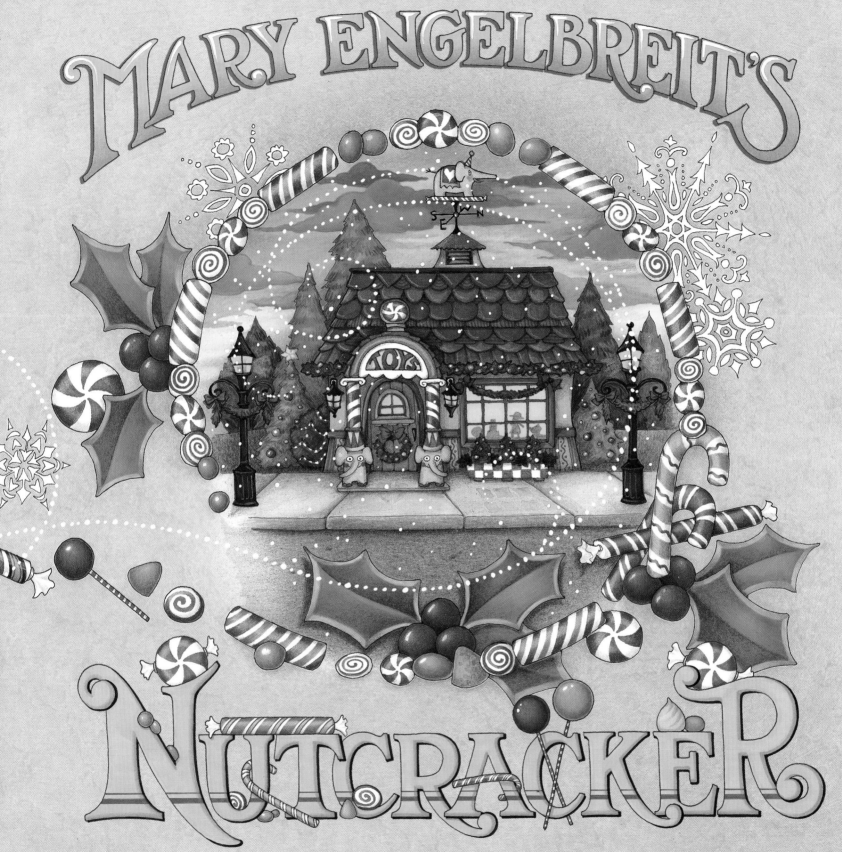

MARY ENGELBREIT'S

NUTCRACKER

HARPER

An Imprint of HarperCollinsPublishers

DROSSELMEYER'S TOY SHOP

Once upon a time, the Nutcracker had been placed under a terrible spell that changed him from a handsome prince to an ugly thing. He believed that the Mouse King's spell meant that no one could ever learn to love him.

So he was surprised when the toymaker, Drosselmeyer, took him from the shelf, saying, "You will be the perfect gift for my niece, Marie."

As their car rolled into the night, the Nutcracker wondered
what was in store.
After a long ride, they stopped in front of a lovely house all
aglow with festive light. Before you could say "Merry Christmas,"
the Nutcracker was inside.

Marie and her little brother, Fritz, waited by the beautiful
Christmas tree in the living room, excited to greet their uncle.
A hush fell over the guests as the toymaker unveiled his gifts.

Drosselmeyer gave Fritz a box of magnificent toy soldiers. Turning
to Marie, he presented two large dolls, Harlequin and Columbine.

They danced and twirled with each other until the guests were nearly dizzy from watching.

And then, while the others marveled at the two dolls, Uncle Drosselmeyer gave Marie the Nutcracker.

She loved him at first sight, but Fritz was jealous that his sister had received another gift. When he cracked the Nutcracker's head trying to open a nut, Fritz shouted, "Who cares? He's the ugliest thing I've ever seen!"

Marie cried as she bound the Nutcracker's head with a silky red ribbon. "You are not ugly to me," she whispered, putting him to rest under the Christmas tree.

Later she crept down the stairs to see if he was well.
In the dreamy quiet of night, she soon fell asleep. . . .

Boom! Boom! Marie was
awakened with a terrible fright.
Drosselmeyer sat on the booming
grandfather clock, sprinkling
magic into the air. Below him, the
floor began to shake.

Out from the darkness came the very fierce Mouse King,
wearing a golden crown and waving his sword. Marie was
so frightened, she fell and bumped her knee.

The Nutcracker leapt to her defense and led the fight,
shouting, "Charge!" But the Mouse King was strong.

Just when all seemed hopeless, Marie threw her shoe at the Mouse King and saved the Nutcracker.

The Nutcracker seized a silver sword from one of Fritz's toy soldiers and challenged the Mouse King one last time. Their battle was fierce.

Yet, by the stroke of midnight, the Nutcracker had claimed his victory and the spell was broken. The Nutcracker was himself again.

Now a handsome prince, the Nutcracker whispered, "Thank you, dear Marie." When he gave her the Mouse King's golden crown, her heart swelled with happiness. Then he asked, "Will you come to Toyland, my kingdom? I want you to love it as I do."

Snowflakes spun around them as they flew
through the cold night into a land of warmth
and sunshine.

They passed through a forest where golden fruit grew on every branch and the smell of Christmas and candy floated around them. Soon they came upon a little gathering of dancers who played reed flutes so sweetly, each note seemed to be made of sugar.

Then Marie saw a beautiful lady coming toward them from a distance.

"This is the Sugar Plum Fairy," the Prince said. "She watched over Toyland while I was under the spell."

Flute music floated in the air as the Sugar Plum Fairy led them across the kingdom to the Prince's gingerbread castle.

They feasted on
chocolates,
gingersnaps,
and cakes.

As they ate, dancers from every kingdom entertained them.

At last the Prince asked Marie to
dance with him. As the moon glimmered
above them, she whispered, "I love you,
my Nutcracker."

When Marie woke the next morning, she was back in her own bed, and her Nutcracker was nowhere to be found. She ran downstairs to search for him and found her Uncle Drosselmeyer. Behind him was her Prince!

The Prince said, "By loving me despite my appearance, you set me free from the Mouse King's spell." He gently took her hand. "If you'll agree, when you are grown, I'll return and make you Queen of Toyland."

And in that magical place, they lived happily ever after.

Mary Engelbreit's Nutcracker

Copyright © 2011 by Mary Engelbreit Ink

All rights reserved. Manufactured in China. No part of this book may be used or
reproduced in any manner whatsoever without written permission except in the
case of brief quotations embodied in critical articles and reviews.

For information address HarperCollins Children's Books, a division of HarperCollins
Publishers, 195 Broadway, New York, NY 10007.

www.harpercollinschildrens.com

Library of Congress Cataloging-in-Publication Data
Engelbreit, Mary.

Mary Engelbreit's Nutcracker / by Mary Engelbreit. — 1st ed.

p.   cm.

Summary: In this retelling of the original 1816 German story, a nutcracker
under a terrible spell is given to young Marie as a Christmas gift, and when she helps
him defeat the Mouse King, breaking the spell, he takes her to visit his kingdom.

ISBN 978-0-06-222417-0 (paper-over-board edition)

[1. Fairy tales.   2. Christmas—Fiction.]   I. Hoffmann, E. T. A. (Ernst Theodor
Amadeus), 1776–1822. Nussknacker und Mausekönig.   II. Title.   III. Title: Nutcracker.

PZ8.E569Md 2011   2010018438

[E]—dc22   CIP

                                                                              AC

Typography by Jeanne L. Hogle

14 15 16 17 18   SCP   10 9 8 7 6 5 4 3 2 1

❖

First paper-over-board edition, 2014
Also available in a hardcover edition.